EJ
Oelsc
Oelschlager, Vanita

Life is a Bowl of Cherries : a book
of food idioms and silly pictures

All net profits from this book will be donated to

charitable organizations, with a gentle preference towards

people with my husband's disease – multiple sclerosis.

Vanita Oelschlager

Acknowledgments

Many Thanks to:

Robin Hegan

Jennie Levy Smith

Kurt Landefeld

Paul Royer

Mike Blanc

Sheila Tarr

Katherine Y. Hatcher

Elaine Mesek

Gailmarie Fort

Life is a Bowl Full of Cherries
VanitaBooks, LLC
All rights reserved.
© 2011 VanitaBooks, LLC
No part of this book may be reproduced, stored in retrieval systems, or transmitted in any form or
through methods including electronic photocopying, online download, or any other system now known
or hereafter invented – except by reviewers, who may quote brief passages in a review to be printed in a
newspaper or print or online publication – without express written permission from VanitaBooks, LLC.
Text by Vanita Oelschlager.
Illustrations by Robin Hegan.
Design by Jennie Levy Smith,
Trio Design & Marketing Communications Inc.
Printed in China.
ISBN 978-0-9826366-3-3 Hardcover
ISBN 978-0-9826366-2-6 Paperback

www.VanitaBooks.com

written by **Vanita Oelschlager** illustrated by **Robin Hegan**

This book is dedicated with love to all my grandchildren who are all 'the apple of my eye'.
Vanita Oelschlager

This book is dedicated to my Snickle-Pickles.
Robin Hegan

Life is a Bowl Full of Cherries

a book of **food idioms** *and* **silly pictures**

This is a very important person.

"My grandpa was a big cheese in the Army."

Big cheese

Couch potato

I'm planted and I can't get up!

"Billy was a *couch potato* until he got interested in playing basketball."

This is a person who is lazy and lies around on the couch watching TV all day.

Cry over spilt milk

This means to complain about something that has already happened that you can't do anything about.

"So we lost the ballgame – let's not cry over spilt milk."

("Spilt" was the old word for spilled.)

This is an idea that is worth taking
time to think about, something that
will grow in your mind.

"My teacher said I would be a good
doctor: that is *food for thought*."

Food for thought

Sweet tooth

You're having a sweet and enjoyable time.

"Compared to my last job, this one is like a bowl full of cherries."

Life is a bowl
full of cherries

Packed in like sardines!

"The elevator was so full we were packed in like sardines."

When people or things are squashed into a small area,
they can look like sardines (a small fish) in a can.

The whole enchilada

When someone wants it all.

"He wasn't satisfied with part of the land, he wanted the whole enchilada."

One bad apple

One bad person may spoil the whole group.

"The coach kicked him off the team for cheating.
He said, 'One bad apple could spoil the bunch.'"

You can catch
more flies
with honey than
with vinegar

"Ask your mom nicely: remember you can catch more flies with honey than vinegar."

More can be accomplished by being nice (sweet) to someone than by being nasty (sour).

"My tire went flat during the race. That really cooked my goose."

This means that you put an end to your plans or to someone else's plans and nothing can undo it.

Your goose
is cooked

Pie-in-the-sky

"The moon needed a vacation."

"Being an astronaut at 13 is a pie-in-the-sky dream."

This is something you think you can do that is unrealistic.

Hmmm...there is something different about that turkey! I just can't put my feather on it.

Cold turkey

You suddenly stop something that is a habit.

"I stopped playing video games *cold turkey*. I went to the library and got out some good books I would like instead."

"When my sister said I couldn't pass the test and I did, she had to eat her words."

You have to take back what you said and admit that you were wrong.

Eat your words

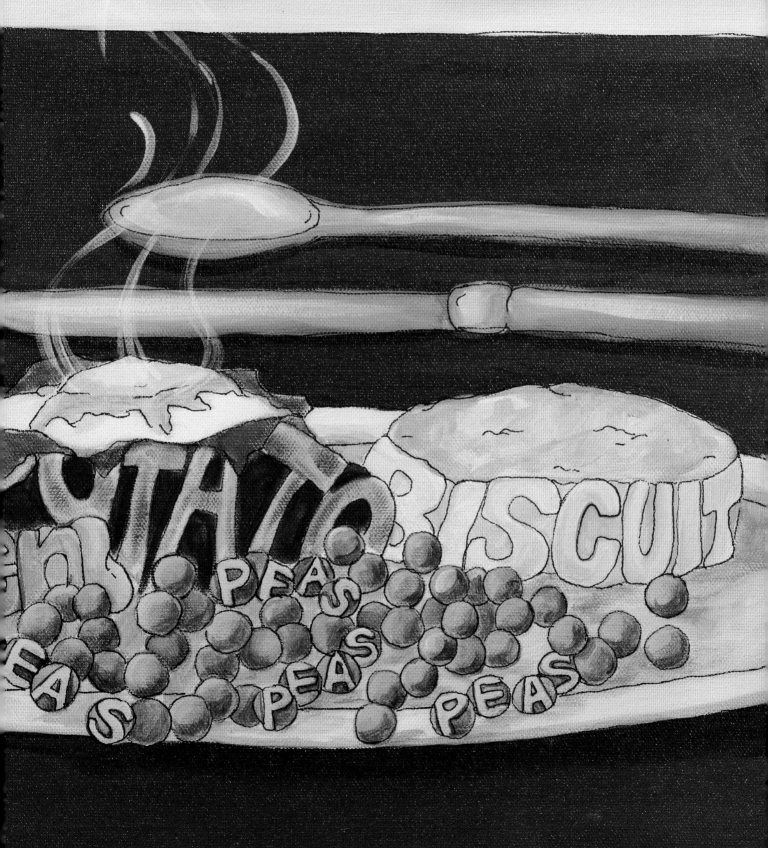

What are idioms?

Every language has "figures of speech", or idioms. They are kind of a short hand way of explaining something unfamiliar or complicated.

The English language has thousands of them. You cannot understand them because the group of words together has little, often nothing, to do with the meanings of the words taken one by one.

Hundreds of years ago, the words might have meant what they said, but today they do not.

In order to understand a language, you must know what the idioms in that language mean. If you try to figure out the meaning of the idiom word by word you're likely to get nowhere – you will get befuddled or confused. You have to know the "hidden" meaning. You need to read between the lines and behind the words.

I am going to show you the "hidden" meaning of two idioms. Maybe you can find out the "hidden" meaning of some other idioms in this book. Idioms often show a sense of humor. They're your language's ticklish spots so learning them can be lots of fun. I hope you'll enjoy them as much as we do.

Food for thought
People have used this idiom since the early 1800s. We think of the mind as a mouth that "chews" not food, but ideas. These ideas are *food for thought.* It is something to be thought over carefully.

One bad apple
Benjamin Franklin had this saying in his famous book *Poor Richard's Almanac* in 1736. It goes back really to the mid-1500s. It is true that if you leave one rotten apple in a barrel it may rot the others. Rottenness seems to spread. This is said about people too. One person with bad behavior in a group can sometimes cause others to go bad.

Vanita Oelschlager is a wife, mother, grandmother, former teacher, caregiver, author, and poet. She was named "Writer in Residence" for the Literacy Program at The University of Akron in 2007. She is a graduate of Mount Union College, Alliance, Ohio, where she is currently a member of the Board of Trustees.

Like two peas in a pod

Robin Hegan grew up in the Laurel Mountains of Pennsylvania where imagination took her and her childhood friends on many great adventures. After graduating from The Pennsylvania State University with a degree in Integrative Arts, Robin resided in Ohio for several years until she and her husband, Matt, decided to return to the mountains of Pennsylvania to raise their children. Robin's illustrations can also be seen in *My Grampy Can't Walk*, *Mother Goose Other Goose* and *Birds of a Feather*. To find out more about Robin, visit www.robinhegan.com.

They both like to make books for children to enjoy."

"The author and the illustrator are like two peas in a pod.

When two people are alike in some ways.